W9-ACS-764

A NOTE TO PARENTS

When your children are ready to "step into reading," giving them the right books is as crucial as giving them the right food to eat. **Step into Reading Books** and STAR WARS® **JEDI READERS** present exciting stories and information reinforced with lively, colorful illustrations that make learning to read fun, satisfying, and worthwhile. They are priced so that acquiring an entire library of them is affordable. And they are beginning readers with a difference—they're written on five levels.

Early Step into Reading Books are designed for brand-new readers, with large type and only one or two lines of very simple text per page. **Step 1 Books** feature the same easy-to-read type as the Early Step into Reading Books, but with more words per page. **Step 2 Books** are both longer and slightly more difficult, while **Step 3 Books** introduce readers to paragraphs and fully developed plot lines. **Step 4 Books** offer exciting fiction and nonfiction for the increasingly independent reader.

The grade levels assigned to the five steps—preschool through kindergarten for the Early Books, preschool through grade 1 for Step 1, grades 1 through 3 for Step 2, grades 2 through 3 for Step 3, and grades 2 through 4 for Step 4—are intended only as guides. Some children move through all five steps very rapidly; others climb the steps over a period of several years. Either way, these books will help your child "step into reading" in style!

www.randomhouse.com/kids
www.starwars.com

Library of Congress Cataloging-in-Publication Data
Venn, Cecilia.
Anakin to the rescue / by Cecilia Venn ; illustrated by Chris Trevas.
p.   cm. — (Jedi readers. A step 2 book)
SUMMARY: On the planet Coruscant, young Anakin Skywalker helps a lost boy find his way home.
ISBN 0-375-80001-8 (trade). — ISBN 0-375-90001-2 (lib. bdg.)
[1. Science fiction.]   I. Trevas, Chris, ill.   II. Title.   III. Series: Jedi readers. Step 2 book.   PZ7.V558An   1999   [Fic]—dc21   98-48536

Printed in the United States of America   10 9 8 7 6 5 4 3 2 1
STEP INTO READING is a registered trademark of Random House, Inc.

JEDI READERS

STAR WARS®

EPISODE I

ANAKIN to the RESCUE

A Step 2 Book

BY CECILIA VENN
ILLUSTRATED BY CHRIS TREVAS

Random House
New York

Anakin walked back and forth.
He was waiting for
his friend Qui-Gon
to come out of the Jedi Temple.
He was waiting to find out
if he could train to be a Jedi.

Anakin thought about

his home on Tatooine.

He thought about his mother.

He missed her.

Anakin stood up.

"I can't wait here anymore,"

he said to himself.

"I will just have a look around.

I will not go far."

Jar Jar saw Anakin

walking away.

He did not want his friend

to get in trouble.

So he followed Anakin.

Anakin walked and walked.
There were
so many shops.
There were
so many creatures.
Jar Jar could not catch up!

Anakin looked up.

He saw a tall, sparkly building.

So did Jar Jar.

Anakin went over bridges.

Anakin went under bridges.

So did Jar Jar.

Anakin walked and walked
until the big, shiny buildings
hid the sky.
Finally, Anakin was ready
to turn back.
He looked all around,
but he could not see
the Jedi Temple.
But he did see Jar Jar!

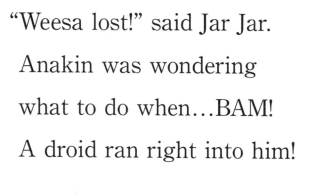

"Weesa lost!" said Jar Jar.
Anakin was wondering
what to do when...BAM!
A droid ran right into him!

The droid spun in a circle.

"There's no place like...BEEP!"

said the droid.

"No place...BEEP!"

A very little boy was with
the droid.
He was crying.
He grabbed Jar Jar's leg.
"Help, big froggy man,"
he said.

"Who are you?" asked Anakin.

"I am Finn," said the boy.

"My nanny droid is broken.

I want my mommy!

I want to go home!"

"I know how you feel,"

said Anakin.

"But you are very lucky.

I can fix your droid!"

Suddenly, the droid sped off.

"Catch it!" Anakin yelled.

He grabbed Finn's hand

and they ran.

Jar Jar ran, too.

They followed the droid
into a building.
Inside, they saw *many* droids.
But they all looked the same!
"Which isa the one?" said Jar Jar.

"We're in a hall of mirrors,"
explained Anakin.
"Follow the sound of the beeps.
We have to find the real droid."

All of the droids were
rolling toward a doorway.
"This way!"
shouted Anakin.

The droid rolled outside.

Anakin, Finn, and Jar Jar

raced after it.

Its head spun round and round.

Then it zipped into an airbus

that was docked at a bus stop.

Anakin and Finn stepped out

onto the dock.

It was very high up!

Anakin was a little scared.

But then he remembered
his mom's words.
"Be brave, Anakin."
So he and Finn kept going
and got on the airbus.

But Jar Jar was afraid.

"Jump, Jar Jar!" Anakin yelled.

"Meesa no big jumper,"

said Jar Jar.

"Thatz for frogs."

The airbus began to leave.

Whooosh!

Jar Jar lost his balance.

He fell forward...

...and landed in the airbus,
right on top of Anakin.
"Oooof," said Anakin.
"Oyi! Meesa okay dokey,"
said Jar Jar.
Finn giggled.

The airbus pulled up to
the next docking bay.
The runaway droid
zoomed off the airbus.
"Look!" said Finn.
"There it goes!"

The droid rolled into
a busy intersection.

Anakin and Finn ran
along the sidewalk.
But Jar Jar ran into
the middle of the road!

"Outta the way, swamp-man,"
yelled an ugly alien.
Anakin yanked Jar Jar
out of the road.

"The droid is going into
a trash chute!"
shouted Anakin.
Anakin, Jar Jar, and Finn
followed it.

They all slid down

the trash chute.

Clank!

They landed on

a junk pile.

The junk pile shook and beeped.

Out popped the droid!

Kachiiiing! Zzzzirrr! PFFFSSSTT!

The droid's eyes closed.

"Meesa tink we got it now!"

Jar Jar said.

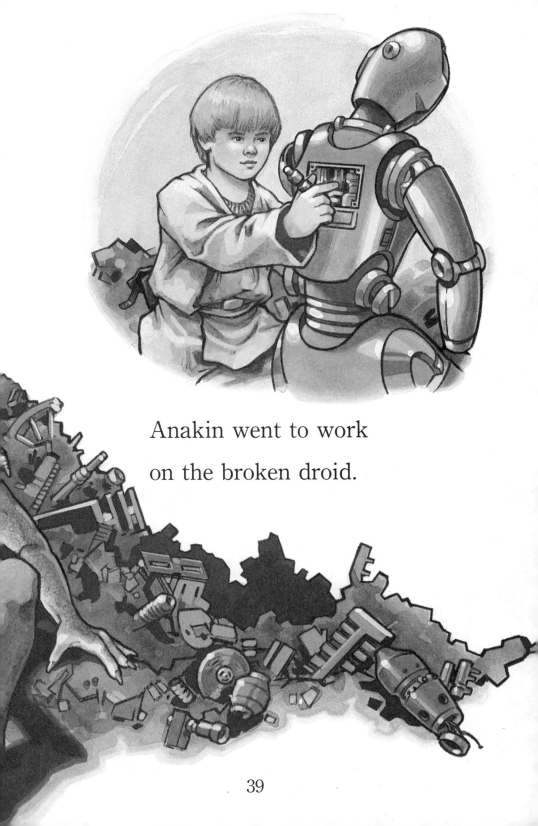

Anakin went to work

on the broken droid.

"Look!" Finn screamed.

Dozens of spider-roaches were
coming at them!

Slurp!

Jar Jar's tongue shot out
and scooped one up.

"Heydey ho! Snack for meesa!"
said Jar Jar.

The droid's eyes popped open.

"Hurray! It's fixed," said Finn.

"There's no place like home,"
said the droid.

The droid led them
to Finn's home.
Finn jumped into
his mother's arms.
He told her what happened.

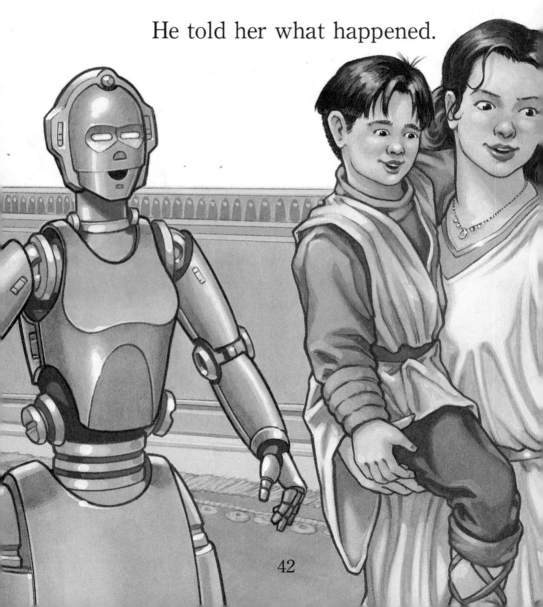

Finn's mom hugged Anakin.
"Your mother would be
very proud of you,"
she said.
"Now let *me* help *you*
get back to the Temple."

A droid drove Anakin
and Jar Jar to the Temple.
Qui-Gon was waiting.
He looked worried.
"Weesa in big doo doo!"
said Jar Jar.

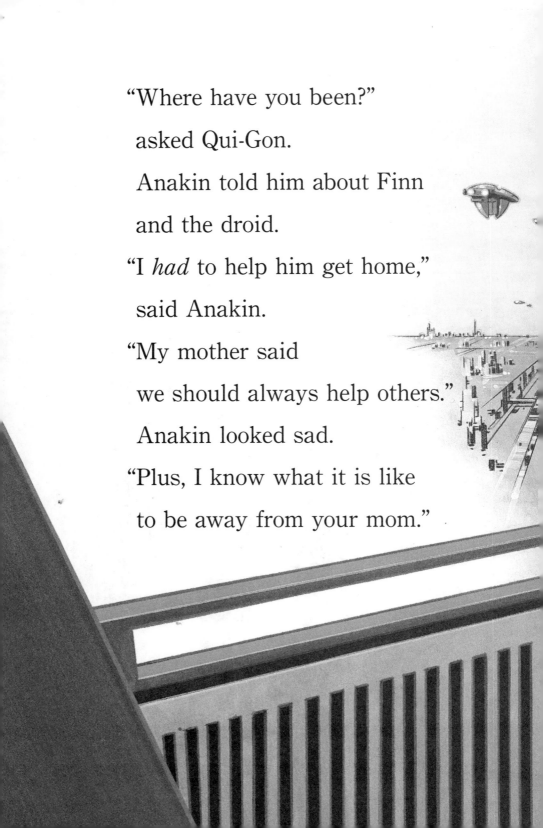

"Where have you been?"
asked Qui-Gon.
Anakin told him about Finn
and the droid.
"I *had* to help him get home,"
said Anakin.
"My mother said
we should always help others."
Anakin looked sad.
"Plus, I know what it is like
to be away from your mom."

"I understand,"
Qui-Gon answered.
He put his arm around Anakin.
"You did what a Jedi would do."